The Old Man & His Door

by **Gary Soto**

illustrations by **Joe Cepeda**

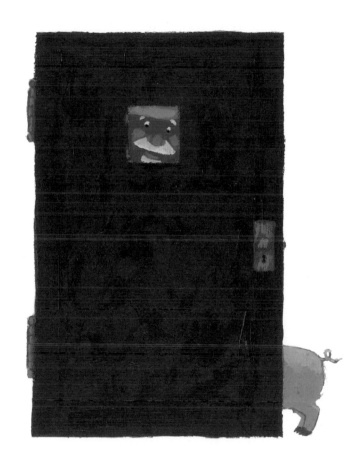

G. P. Putnam's Sons   New York

Para Francisco y Apolonia Soto,
mis Abuelitos. –G. S.

For my family. –J. C.

Glossary of Spanish Terms

la puerta	lah PWEHR-tah	the door
el puerco	el PWEHR-koh	the pig
el viejo	el vee-EH-hoh	the old man
la vieja	lah vee-EH-hah	the old woman
la comadre	lah ko-MAH-dray	the neighbor
sí	see	yes
entiendo	en-tee-EN-doh	I understand
pues	pwehs	well; well then
¿Qué pasa?	kay pah-sah	What's going on?
pobrecita	poh-bray-SEE-tah	poor little girl
tan-tan	tahn-tahn	knock-knock
por favor	pohr fah-VOHR	please
ay, dios	i DEE-ohs	oh, God
ayúdame	i-YOO-dah-may	help me
mil gracias	meel GRAH-see-ahs	a thousand thanks
mira	MEE-rah	look
muchísimas gracias	moo-CHEE-see-mahs GRAH-see-ahs	thanks very much
de nada	day nah-dah	it was nothing (you're welcome)
el huevo	el HWAY-voh	the egg

Text copyright © 1996 by Gary Soto. Illustrations copyright © 1996 by Joe Cepeda
All rights reserved. This book, or parts thereof, may not be reproduced in any form without
permission in writing from the publisher. G. P. Putnam's Sons, a division of The Putnam & Grosset Group,
200 Madison Avenue, New York, NY 10016. G. P. Putnam's Sons, Reg. U.S. Pat. & Tm. Off.
Published simultaneously in Canada. Printed in Hong Kong by South China Printing Co. (1988) Ltd.
Book designed by Patrick Collins. Text set in Aurelia.
Library of Congress Cataloging-in-Publication Data
Soto, Gary.   The old man and his door / by Gary Soto; illustrations by Joe Cepeda.   p.   cm.
Summary: Misunderstanding his wife's instructions, an old man sets out for a party with a door on his back.
[1. Doors–Fiction. 2. Parties–Fiction.] I. Cepeda, Joe, ill. II. Title.   PZ7.S7242O1   1996   [E]–dc20   94-27085 CIP AC
ISBN 0-399-22700-8

1   3   5   7   9   10   8   6   4   2

First Impression

In Mexico there's a little song that goes like this: "La puerta. El puerco.
There's no difference to el viejo." That's because to a viejo, *an old man,*
they sound so much alike – especially if he's not listening carefully.
Of course in Spanish "puerta" means "door," and "puerco" means "pig."
So, young or old, if you don't listen carefully, it can get you in trouble!

This is the story of an old man in a little village who was
good at working in the garden, but terrible at listening to his wife.

He could grow the biggest tomatoes and the hottest of hot *chiles*. His chickens were large and white, and his pigs as plump as water balloons.

But whenever his wife called him, he would hurry into his garden and pick up a hoe, pretending to be busy. Later, over dinner, he'd say, "*Vieja*, I didn't hear you."

One Saturday, while he was giving their dog, Coco, a bath on the porch, his wife came out of the house dressed in her best clothes. She was off to her *comadre*'s for a barbecue.

"I don't want you to be late, *viejo*," she warned.

"I won't," he promised. "Just let me finish here."

But right then Coco jumped from the tub and ran away, with a mountain of suds on his back. The old man dropped the soap and scrub brush and ran after him. They circled the house three times and the avocado tree nine times, with the chickens and pigs stampeding behind.

"I want you to bring *el puerco*," the wife screamed each time he came around the house. "Did you hear me? *El puerco*. Don't forget to bring the pig!"

"*Sí. Entiendo.* I hear you!" He panted as he ran, not really listening. Finally Coco ran into the tomato vines, where the old man caught him and carried him back to the tub.

The wife left, dizzy from watching. She closed the gate behind
her and set off up the road.

The old man started Coco on another bath. When he finished he scratched his head and said to himself, "*Pues*, I don't know why my wife wants me to bring a *puerta*."

But he didn't dare argue. He shrugged and unscrewed the front door. Then he heaved it onto his shoulders and headed up the street.

After a mile he stopped to rest, near a small, shabby house. Out front was a little girl taking care of her baby sister, who was crying. *"¿Qué pasa?"* the old man asked. "What's the matter?"

"The baby is bored," the girl answered. "She has nothing to play
with except her fingers and the hole in her pocket."

"*Pobrecita*," he said, as he combed her soft hair with his fingers.

Suddenly the old man had an idea. He took the baby into his arms
and brought her to the door. He placed the baby on one side, and

himself on the other. Together they played peek-a-boo and "*tan-tan,*
who's there?" until the baby gave him a kiss and gurgled happily.

The old man continued on his way to the barbecue, whistling and playing kick-the-rock. The road was empty and the blue sky as wide as a hat.

Then, as he passed under a tree, the door bumped a beehive hanging from a vine.

All around him buzzed a swarm of angry bees.

"*Ay, ay, ay,*" he shouted, and ran until his legs grew tired. "These bees are too fast!" Panting, he lay down with the door on top of him, until the bees buzzed past. Then, slowly, he opened the peephole and saw only a square patch of sky.

"That was close!" he said, and rose to his feet. The old man looked at the beehive and imagined the honey inside. No point in wasting it, he thought. So he drained the honey into his hat, balanced it on the door, and continued on his way.

Soon a ragged goose dropped from the sky and landed on the door, now heavier by the weight of a few scruffy feathers.

"*Por favor*, rest on my door," the old man offered. "Ride as long as you want."

The ragged goose honked gratefully. She rode for a mile, and when the old man stopped to rest, the goose flapped her wings and flew away. The old man wiped his brow and looked back at the door.

"What's this?" he asked, light in his eyes. He felt the weight of a big egg in his palm.

"*Ay, dios,*" he said beaming. "I'm a lucky man!"

He started off again with the door on his shoulders. But before
long he heard shouts coming from the lake. He shaded his eyes
and looked toward the water.

"*¡Ayúdame!*" a boy screamed. "Help me!"

The old man ran down to the lake. He threw the door into the water and paddled out to the drowning boy. He hauled him onto the door, where they both panted with relief. A turtle wriggled from the old man's shirt, and a fish jumped from his pocket.

The boy thanked him a thousand times. *"Mil gracias,"* he said.
"Just promise me," the old man said as he steered toward shore,
"you'll listen to your parents and stay dry until you can swim."
On land the old man brushed a wet leaf from the boy's face.
Then he lifted a fish from the boy's shirt. *"Míra,* another one,"
he said, admiring its gleaming scales. He placed it in his pocket.

The old man waved good-bye and balanced the dripping door on his shoulders. Now he hurried back to the road, because he knew he was late to the barbecue. His wife would be angry.

But he stopped after only a few minutes, when he saw a young man trying to load furniture into a wagon.

"Here, let's use this," the old man said, patting the door.
He propped it against the wagon so they could use it as a ramp.
Then they loaded chairs and tables, and a large piano that
tinkled as they pushed.

"Muchísimas gracias," the young man said.

"*De nada.* You're welcome," the old man replied. "I never knew a door had so many uses."

Together they placed the door on the old man's shoulders. The young man balanced two watermelons on either side. "These are from my garden," he said.

The old man hurried along with his gifts and finally arrived at
the *comadre*'s house. The barbecue was in the yard. There was music
playing, and a donkey piñata hung from the tree.

"I'm here!" he announced. The door slid from his shoulders.

"*¡Ay, dios!*" cried his wife. "What are you doing with the door?"

"*Pues*, you told me to bring it," he said, wiping his brow. "It was hard work."

"I said to bring *el puerco*, not *la puerta*!" She wheeled around to her *comadre*. "He never listens to me. I ask him to bring the pig, and he brings the door!"

The old man had to laugh. He took the egg from his pocket and said, "But look what else I brought."

"*¿Un huevo?*" she said with surprise.

"*Sí.* An egg, and some honey, a fish, and these watermelons! And even this," he said, and gave his wife the kiss from the baby.

"You brought all this?" His wife blushed.

"*Sí.* Let me tell you how it happened…"

"Tell us over dinner," the *comadre* interrupted kindly.

They barbecued the fish, boiled the egg, sliced the watermelons,

made a table of the door, and placed the honey hat in the center.

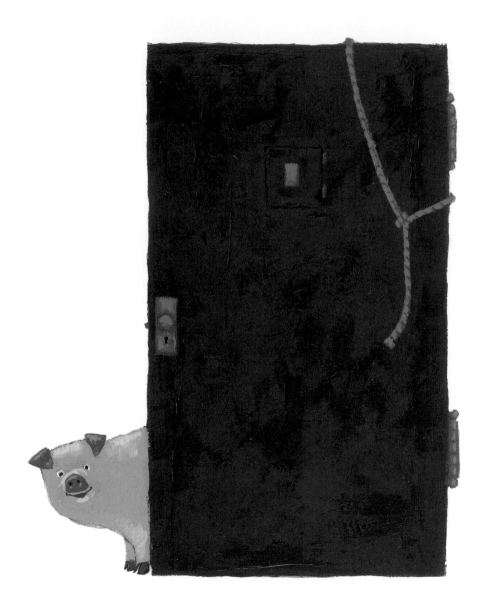

La puerta. El puerco. There's no difference to *el viejo*!